Our Friend, Old Bob

Written by John Parsons

Illustrated by Margaret Power

Contents

Meet the Characters

Old Bob

A homeless man who cannot read or write.

Mr Jermyn

The principal of Southwold school.

Claire

A student at Southwold school.

Mrs O'Driscoll

Claire's mother.

Dear Reader

Once, I was waiting for a bus. Sitting next to me in the bus shelter were two old homeless people. They were scruffy and unkempt – but I was amazed when I heard what they were talking about: the plays of William Shakespeare!

I wondered how they had become homeless – and realised that you can never judge people by the way they look!

John Parsons
Author

The Lea Valley

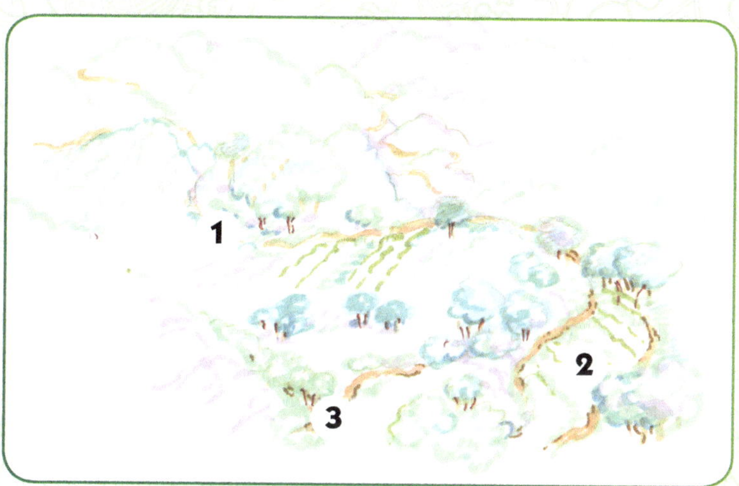

1. The road from Southwold
2. The ravine
3. The road to Northmount

1 A Fair Deal

No matter how hard she tried, Mrs Kemp, the school secretary, found it difficult to keep her curious eyes focused on the computer keyboard in front of her.

Her gaze flicked over her red-rimmed spectacles towards the row of chairs along the wall of the Southwold School office. She wrinkled her nose involuntarily. There, squirming in the middle chair, nursing a crumpled supermarket plastic bag on his lap, sat a dishevelled, unkempt man.

"I don't know who he is," she'd whispered into the telephone a few minutes earlier. "He says his name is Bob, and he wants to see you."

Mr Jermyn, the principal, had agreed to see Bob. "I just have to finish these reports," Mr Jermyn had said. "Can you ask him to wait for a few minutes, please?"

"Mr Jermyn will see you in a moment," Mrs Kemp had told Bob, wondering what he could possibly want to speak to the principal about. She noticed an old scar beneath his grizzly whiskers.

Bob had nodded, mumbled something and wriggled nervously in his chair. He looked like he would be more comfortable sitting at a bus stop or on a park bench.

Mrs Kemp tried not to stare at the scruffy man. Nevertheless, she couldn't help flicking her eyes upwards once more and, to her alarm, she saw Bob looking straight back at her. She forced herself to smile, and Bob responded with a grin, revealing a mouthful of gaping holes where his teeth should have been.

The man plunged a grimy hand into his crumpled supermarket bag, rustling around its contents noisily.

"Chocolate?" he asked, offering Mrs Kemp a half-eaten block that he'd retrieved from his bag.

Mrs Kemp tried not to shudder.

"No, thank you. Just had breakfast," she said, smiling weakly.

Bob shrugged his shoulders nonchalantly. "Just about to have mine," he said. He wiped the chocolate on his overcoat, and popped two squares into his mouth.

Mrs Kemp tried to concentrate on the agenda for the staff meeting that she was supposed to be typing into the computer, but the sound of a satisfied Bob noisily sucking and swirling chocolate around his mouth was too distracting.

Just when Mrs Kemp was wondering how much longer she would have to put up with the man, the door marked "Principal" swung open and Mr Jermyn strode over to the row of chairs.

"Hello," said Mr Jermyn, looking Bob up and down. "I'm Mr Jermyn, the principal. How can we help you?"

Bob flashed what few teeth he had, stained with chocolate, and held out his hand. Mrs Kemp, who

had been keeping a furtive eye on proceedings, was impressed that Mr Jermyn didn't flinch. He took Bob's hand and shook it.

Under Mr Jermyn's gaze, Bob shuffled uncomfortably. "I have a question," he said, his eyes firmly fixed on the office carpet.

Mr Jermyn smiled helpfully, and raised his eyebrows expectantly.

Bob glanced over at Mrs Kemp and rustled his plastic bag nervously. "It's a personal question," he added.

"Right," said Mr Jermyn, catching Mrs Kemp's eye. He looked at his watch. "Well, I do have a minute before my next ... aah, my next appointment, don't I, Mrs Kemp?"

Mrs Kemp shuffled some papers on her desk, pretending to look for the imaginary appointment. "Yes, Mr Jermyn," she replied. "Just a minute."

"You'd better come in," said Mr Jermyn, waving Bob towards the principal's door.

Bob looked nervous.

"Been a while since you've been summoned to the principal's office, eh?" joked Mr Jermyn, trying to put his visitor at ease.

Bob nodded. He and his plastic bag shuffled noisily towards Mr Jermyn's office.

Mr Jermyn followed Bob and, with a backwards glance at Mrs Kemp, he raised his eyebrows and shut the door.

Mrs Kemp heard a muffled conversation taking place behind the principal's door. She decided to give Bob and Mr Jermyn two minutes before she dialled the extension that connected through to Mr Jermyn's phone. She heard a ring behind the door and Mr Jermyn's voice crackled down the line.

"Hello?" he said.

"Your next appointment, Mr Jermyn," she said conspiratorially. "I hope you don't mind that I've made you spend two minutes with that man," she whispered.

But, to her surprise, Mr Jermyn didn't play along with the ruse.

"It's perfectly fine, Mrs Kemp," said Mr Jermyn. "Can you ask ... ah, whoever it is I'm scheduled to see to make another appointment, please?"

The phone line went dead and Mrs Kemp replaced her receiver, looking startled. She'd fully expected Bob to be politely ushered out of the principal's office and pointed firmly back to his park bench or his bus stop, or wherever he spent his days. Instead, the principal of Southwold School seemed to be paying some attention to whatever it was he had to say.

Mr Jermyn looked at Bob. His unshaven whiskers, his tousled and unwashed hair and his leathery skin, hardened by years of living rough, made it virtually impossible to guess his age.

"Fifty," answered Bob. "Well, close as I can tell."

"Fifty," repeated Mr Jermyn, writing the number down on a sheet of paper. "And do you have a postal address, Mr ... er, Bob?"

Bob looked blank. He shrugged his shoulders.

"We'll just put down 'care of Southwold School' for the moment," smiled Mr Jermyn. He put down his pen and fixed Bob with a curious look.

"Are you sure you want to do this?" he said. "If I'm willing to give this a try, I want to know that you will agree to do the right thing, Bob, and behave properly. This is a school – my school – and there's no doubt my reputation will be well and truly on the line if we try this."

Bob nodded and looked Mr Jermyn directly in the eye. The principal was struck by how clear and determined Bob's expression was.

“All I’m asking for is a chance,” he said, with a pleading tone in his voice. “A second chance.”

“OK,” nodded Mr Jermyn. “But you must promise faithfully to follow the rules. My rules. Is that a fair deal?”

Bob nodded and his face broke into a broad smile.

“Let’s not get too excited,” warned Mr Jermyn. “There’s a lot of bureaucracy we have to wade through before we can start.”

Bob pointed to his scuffed and muddy leather boots, which were two sizes too big for his feet.

“Where I sleep, there’s always plenty of puddles,” he said. “I’m used to wading.”

2 A New Classmate

Mrs O'Driscoll had a concerned expression on her face as she read the letter that her daughter, Claire, had brought home after school.

She rattled the letter sharply, as if that would somehow rearrange the words into something that was less perturbing. But, when she read it again, the information it contained still did not impress her.

Claire and her school friends, Chelsea and Thomas, sat at the kitchen table, sipping a glass of milk each.

"What does it say, Mum?" asked Claire.

"I don't know that I'm very impressed with this idea," replied her mother, pursing her lips. "It simply doesn't seem right, somehow."

Claire pushed back her chair and wandered over to her mother's side, peering at the letter.

Mrs O'Driscoll read the letter aloud.

"After extensive consultation with the town's education authority and the department of social services, Southwold School has decided to offer Mr Christiansen a trial period as an adult student in the school's literacy and reading program. Due to personal circumstances, Mr Christiansen has been illiterate all his life, but we applaud his courageous decision to try and learn to read and write.

I can assure all parents that Mr Christiansen will be closely supervised at all times and, as Southwold School principal, I sincerely hope that he will make the most of the second chance we are offering him. I also hope that you will support our efforts to help Mr Christiansen.
Yours sincerely

Mr Jermyn."

Mrs O'Driscoll looked at her daughter. Claire seemed puzzled.

"That must be Old Bob," piped up her friend Thomas. "I didn't know he had a surname."

"Old Bob?" frowned Mrs O'Driscoll. "You don't mean to say you already know this fellow?"

"Mr Jermyn and our teacher, Miss Penfold, introduced him to the class last week," said Chelsea.

"They wanted to see if he would fit in. He seemed a little scared, but most new kids are, I guess." Claire looked at her mother. "He did seem nice," she added. "He offered us chocolate."

"I hope you didn't take it," said Mrs O'Driscoll.

"No," said Claire ruefully. "It did look a little bit furry."

"He did say it looked better when he found it," added Thomas brightly.

Mrs O'Driscoll shuddered and shook her head.

Two weeks passed. Miss Penfold made sure that the reading groups in her classroom were all fully occupied with the books they'd collected from the book box. Then she went and sat with Old Bob. His knees were jammed awkwardly under the desk that the school had found for him, and he looked like a nervous patient waiting in a dentist's reception room.

When he gave a frightened smile, and showed off his missing teeth, Miss Penfold realised he probably hadn't been to a dentist for the last three or four decades either.

"OK, Bob, we're going to start with the most important sentence you'll ever need to know," she said reassuringly. Miss Penfold picked up one of the freshly sharpened pencils that sat on his desk and slowly wrote out four words on the pristine sheet of paper in front of Old Bob.

"Do you know what that says?" she smiled.

Old Bob scratched his head. "What's for lunch?" he said hopefully.

Miss Penfold chuckled and shook her head. "I suppose that might be a more important sentence," she agreed. "But this one says something completely different."

Old Bob looked at the teacher quizzically.

"My – name – is – Bob," said Miss Penfold, moving her finger and pointing to each word.

"Really?" said Bob, winking. "That's incredible. So is mine." He turned his attention to the strange, unfamiliar squiggles on the piece of paper and slowly moved his finger along, just like Miss Penfold had done.

"My name is Bob," he repeated gravely. He flicked his eyes up at Miss Penfold with an immense look of satisfaction.

"That's a great way to start any story," he said with a nod of his head. "What happens next?"

Miss Penfold shrugged her shoulders. "It's your story, Bob," she smiled.

"How's it going with our adult learner?" enquired Mr Jermyn during lunchtime in the staffroom.

"He's a character," replied Miss Penfold, smiling. "But he has determination and a willingness to succeed, I'll give him that."

"Does he remember anything from the little time he did spend at school?" asked Mr Jermyn.

"A few things," said Miss Penfold. "We're working

on letter sounds and letter combinations. If he sticks with it, he'll do OK."

"What about the other kids?" said Mr Jermyn. "I've had a few parents ring up to make sure that their own children's reading time isn't suffering."

"That won't happen," Miss Penfold assured her principal. "You know I make sure that every student in my class receives all the help they need, whether they're eleven or fifty."

"Good work, Miss Penfold," nodded Mr Jermyn.

It took a few weeks for Old Bob to feel comfortable being part of classroom life, but Miss Penfold was pleased with his progress as he slowly learnt to read and write.

After Mr Jermyn politely suggested that he might want to use the gymnasium showers each morning, Old Bob began to arrive for class freshly scrubbed and eager. One day, after Mrs Kemp had been sent down to the local charity shop, a clean set of clothes appeared on a coathanger outside the showers and

Old Bob spent the rest of the day looking as pleased as punch, even though his new trousers were a little baggy and his nearly new shoes gave him blisters.

"I have the same problem," commented Claire, when she noticed Old Bob gingerly hobbling towards his desk the next morning. "My mum always buys me the wrong-sized shoes. Says I'll grow into them."

Old Bob grinned at Claire.

"These'll be fine," he said. "Just takes a bit of getting used to, after ten years in the same comfy old boots."

Claire's friend Thomas looked impressed. "Ten years!" he said. "Didn't you *ever* take them off?"

"Takes me so long to do up my shoelaces, once they're tied, they stay tied," replied Old Bob.

Miss Penfold even bought Old Bob a roll of stick-on clothing labels. Old Bob laboriously wrote his own name on each one of them, before sticking them on the inside of his new clothes the next morning.

"That's your first information writing assignment completed," Miss Penfold said. "Well done."

As the weeks, then months, passed, Old Bob became a familiar face around Southwold School. He worked diligently during literacy classes, and joined in when the other students played outside during interval or at lunchtime. As the goalie of the school's soccer team quickly found out, when Old Bob kicked off his shoes, he was a good soccer player.

But even though Old Bob found that he was fitting in well with his teachers and classmates, he noticed that some of the parents weren't so friendly towards him. He'd been living rough long enough to notice when someone was avoiding his gaze or was muttering something to their neighbour, casting glances in his direction. He'd grown used to it over the years. But it still hurt, just a little bit, when more fortunate people treated him like he shouldn't really be there.

3 A Helping Hand

Mr Jermyn picked up the telephone that was buzzing insistently on his desk. He knew exactly who would be waiting impatiently outside, and he wasn't looking forward to this morning's appointment.

"Mrs O'Driscoll and the other parents to see you," came Mrs Kemp's voice. "Shall I send them in?"

"I'll pop out," said Mr Jermyn.

He swung open the principal's door and smiled his widest smile at the concerned parents huddled together on the office chairs.

"Come in, come in," he beamed, motioning towards his door with an outstretched arm. "I think we have enough chairs in my office."

The parents trooped silently into the office, led by Mrs O'Driscoll.

When they had all settled into their chairs, Mr Jermyn smiled at the parents expectantly.

"We're concerned about this homeless fellow," started Mrs O'Driscoll. "It's not right that, just because someone was lazy the first time they went to school, they should be allowed to ..."

Mr Jermyn held up his hand.

"Mrs O'Driscoll," he said firmly. "I appreciate that you and some of the other parents are not entirely comfortable with having Old Bob in your children's classroom. But let me assure you, laziness is not something that this man could ever be accused of."

"He sleeps in a bus shelter!" said Mrs O'Driscoll. "I've seen him there, sleeping under newspapers while I'm on my way to work."

"I'm sure that Mr Christiansen would quite happily go to work if someone offered him employment," sighed Mr Jermyn. "But work is not easy to get these days – and when you can't read or write, it's doubly difficult to find."

Mrs O'Driscoll looked troubled. "I'm really not happy that my daughter, Claire, has a homeless person in her class. Something's just not right."

"I agree, Mrs O'Driscoll," said Mr Jermyn. He looked across the table at Mrs O'Driscoll. "It's not right that anyone in our society should have to sleep in a bus shelter. And it's not right that someone, through no fault of their own, has missed out on the chance to learn to read and write. And it's not right," he added firmly, "that people who are more fortunate should want to deny him the second chance we can give him."

Mrs O'Driscoll looked downcast.

"I know that you're concerned for your daughter," continued Mr Jermyn soothingly. "And I can assure you that Old Bob is actually a nice chap. We just need to look past the old clothes and the scruffy hair."

"And the raggedy old supermarket bag," added Mrs O'Driscoll.

"And the raggedy old supermarket bag," nodded Mr Jermyn. "But if we look past all that, Old Bob's a human being, just like you and me. Let's give him the chance he deserves. At least until his trial period is over."

Mrs O'Driscoll, along with the other parents, reluctantly nodded.

"In August, we'll re-evaluate Mr Christiansen's place in school," said Mr Jermyn. "That's only six weeks away, so can we at least give him until then to prove himself?"

Miss Penfold clapped her hands for attention. A sea of eager young faces, and one old, slightly whiskery one, looked up from their work.

"I have some exciting news," she said. "Next week, we're going on a class excursion."

The classroom broke out into an excited buzz.

"On Tuesday, we're going to borrow the school's minibus and drive over to Northmount to visit the newspaper office there. We'll learn all about how a newspaper is written, designed, printed, distributed and used."

The students in the class looked at each other excitedly. Northmount was an hour's drive westward, through the twisting, turning Lea Valley.

Old Bob put his hand up hesitantly.

"Yes?" said Miss Penfold.

"Will they mind if we take some newspaper samples?" he said. "Those night-time winds have been getting quite a bit colder lately."

Miss Penfold and Mr Jermyn finished their meeting. Miss Penfold walked out of the principal's office and nodded to Mrs Kemp.

"Everything OK?" asked Mrs Kemp.

"It will be soon," said Miss Penfold.

Mrs Kemp's phone shrilled. She waved as Miss Penfold headed back to her classroom, and picked up the receiver.

"Yes, Mr Jermyn. I'll do that right away."

Claire, Thomas and Chelsea were sharing a table with Old Bob. They were taking it in turns to read passages from a picture book. Old Bob enjoyed reading aloud with his classmates and, even though Old Bob's books were less complicated than the ones the children were

usually assigned, they enjoyed helping Old Bob work through the stories.

Suddenly, the intercom above the whiteboard crackled into life and Mrs Kemp's voice floated throughout the classroom.

"Would Old Bob ... I mean Mr Christiansen ... please report to the principal's office immediately."

A loud "oooh" sounded throughout the classroom, as the children turned to stare at their classmate. Being summoned to the principal's office usually meant you were in trouble. What had Old Bob been caught doing?

Old Bob looked guilty.

"What have you done?" asked Claire breathlessly.

Old Bob shrugged his shoulders nervously and walked to the classroom door, followed by twenty wide-eyed stares.

Mr Jermyn looked at Old Bob.

"It wasn't me, whatever it was," said Old Bob. "Am I in trouble?"

"No, no," said Mr Jermyn reassuringly. "Not at all."

Old Bob breathed a sigh of relief.

"It's just that ... I need a part-time caretaker for the school, and I was wondering if you'd be interested."

Old Bob jutted his head forward in astonishment and stared at Mr Jermyn.

"It's not the most glamorous job in the world," admitted Mr Jermyn, tapping a pencil on his desk. "And there is a catch."

Old Bob sat back in his chair.

"It's a night caretaker's job," continued Mr Jermyn. "I'm afraid you'd have to sleep over."

Old Bob sat forward again.

"We'd set up an old camp stretcher in the caretaker's shed," said Mr Jermyn. "It wouldn't be much, but ..."

"You mean I could sleep in the caretaker's shed?" said Old Bob. "On a camp stretcher?"

Mr Jermyn nodded.

Old Bob whistled through the gaps in his teeth. He'd never been offered a job before – especially

one with a camp stretcher and a dry shed to shelter from the winter winds.

"Can you start next Wednesday?" asked Mr Jermyn.

Bob wrinkled up his face. For a moment, Mr Jermyn thought Old Bob was about to frown, but then he noticed that his pale old eyes were becoming damp around the edges.

"Thank you, Mr Jermyn," Old Bob said hoarsely.

At interval that afternoon, Mr Jermyn found Miss Penfold in the staffroom.

"Mission accomplished," he said. "I thought he was going to refuse for a moment there – but now Old Bob won't need to take any 'souvenirs' from the Northmount newspaper excursion."

"Thanks, Mr Jermyn," said Miss Penfold. "You didn't tell him that I'd said anything, did you?"

"Not a word," replied Mr Jermyn, sipping his tea. "Now I'd better find someone to help clear out that old caretaker's shed."

4 Old Bob to the Rescue

Tuesday morning rolled around. The light drizzle that fell couldn't dampen the feeling of excitement in the playground.

A buzz of anticipation swirled around the asphalt as Old Bob and the children lined up outside the minibus. With a hiss of compressed air, the doors swung open.

"I love school trips," said Thomas, hitching his backpack on his shoulders.

"Me too," said Claire, clambering aboard.

Old Bob had an anxious look on his face as he found a seat near the back of the minibus and carefully stowed his supermarket bag between his feet. Although he'd spent many hours at bus stops, it had been years and years since he had actually been on a bus. He was strangely silent.

Miss Penfold climbed up the stairs and the doors shut behind her with a gentle swish.

"Good morning, class," she said. "This is our driver, Mr Finlay."

Mr Finlay waved.

"And soon, we'll be on our way to Northmount. Seatbelts fastened, everyone, and enjoy the ride."

Mr Finlay crunched the gears and glanced into the rear-view mirror to check that everyone was sitting safely. He flicked on the windscreen wipers. The bus drew out of the gates of Southwold School and turned left, towards the road that led to the Lea Valley.

The road to Northmount was usually very picturesque, but the drizzle grew heavier as the bus wound its way through the steep valley, which was draped in heavy grey blankets of cloud. Droplets streamed down the outsides of the minibus windows and soon the insides of the windows steamed up.

The children settled back in their seats and contented themselves with drawing faces in the condensation.

Miss Penfold read through a folder of notes she'd brought along and Mr Finlay fiddled with the knob to make the windscreen wipers flick faster and faster.

"Are we there yet?" joked Claire loudly. Everyone on board laughed as the minibus sped towards a long, arching curve.

Little did they know that no one would make it to Northmount that wet, grey morning. And that the next few heart-stopping seconds would be the longest that any of them had ever experienced.

Mrs Kemp shook her head in exasperation. She was trying to complete the forms that needed to be done before Old Bob could be put on the school payroll, but she was finding it extremely difficult. Mr Jermyn was sitting beside her, trying to help.

"How am I supposed to pay someone who doesn't even have a bank account?" she muttered.

"We'll just have to do it the old-fashioned way," said Mr Jermyn. "Remember that stuff they used to have in the old days? Actual money."

"And I can't believe that anyone can get to be fifty years old and not have a tax file number." She set about finding the right form from the tax department and stared at the complex questions that covered the page from head to foot.

"This is going to take ages," she said. "I can't even understand half these questions."

"And you can read," said Mr Jermyn. "Imagine how difficult Old Bob would find this."

Mrs Kemp nodded. She looked out of the window at the incessant rain and shivered.

"I can't imagine sleeping out in this weather," she said. "I do feel sorry for Old Bob."

"Don't feel sorry for him," said Mr Jermyn. "You should feel proud of him for not giving up."

The headlights of the articulated truck speeding around the curve towards the minibus pierced through the gloomy rain. Instantly, Mr Finlay knew something was wrong. They were too near the centre line – way too near. With a flash of horror, he glanced

to the side of the road, desperately looking to see if there was enough room to swerve. The truck lights thundered on towards the minibus. Mr Finlay's instant reaction was to jam his foot on the brake – but he fought his instinct, knowing that sudden braking in this wet weather would cause the minibus to careen wildly out of control.

A deafening roar burst through the valley as the truck driver sounded his horn in a final, terrifying warning. Mr Finlay wrenched the steering wheel over as far as he could. At the last second, through the windscreen, Mr Finlay could see the other driver's white face. And as soon as he did, he knew it was too late.

With a sickening lurch, the squealing tyres lost their grip and slid towards the edge of the road. Gravel sprayed everywhere and the minibus plunged down a ravine.

After the awful, gut-wrenching sound of twisting metal finally coming to rest, the Lea Valley fell horribly silent.

Claire felt someone shaking her violently. She opened her eyes and a splitting pain streaked across her forehead.

"Come on, Claire. We've got to get out of here."

Claire struggled to focus on the face in front of her, but she recognised the voice. Old Bob. Old Bob was wrenching away her seatbelt and then easing her out of the twisted seat.

Somewhere, someone coughed. From another seat came a groan.

Claire felt herself being draped across a pair of arms. Then there was the loud sound of glass breaking and Old Bob's body shook as he kicked furiously at the door.

Suddenly Claire felt splatters of water on her face. It was raining. She smelt the musty smell of damp forest. And then she smelt the acrid smell of something else. Smoke. Thick, oily, black smoke.

Old Bob laid Claire on the wet ground and suddenly she was alone.

"Bob?" she called. "Bob, where are you?" But there was no answer.

The dampness of the ground seeped through Claire's coat and she waited for what seemed like ages. Suddenly she heard the sound of grunting, as someone pushed their way through the undergrowth towards where she lay.

She rolled her head sideways and opened her eyes. To her surprise, she found Thomas was lying on the ground next to her, and behind him, she could see a figure hurrying back down the ravine.

Old Bob.

The smoke became thicker and stung Claire's nostrils. Old Bob seemed to be racing against time as he carried each person to the clearing, before crashing his way back to the wrecked minibus.

Claire struggled to sit up. Across the clearing, she saw Miss Penfold, shivering in shock. Mr Finlay, the driver, lay where Old Bob had gently propped him, a large purple bruise throbbing above his eyes.

Gasping and coughing, Old Bob struggled into the clearing. He carefully laid down the child he'd been carrying and shot a glance over at the other children.

"Last one," he said, another bout of coughing racking his body. "That's everyone."

Another sound rose above the incessant splattering of the rain. It was an ominous crackling, splitting sound, and Old Bob whirled around. A cloud of thick smoke rolled over the clearing.

"Stay here!" he called to the children. "You'll be safe here. Don't move!" And then he disappeared into the bush once more.

5 A Hero Revealed

Amazingly, three days after the crash, there was only one passenger left in hospital. The nurse pointed Mrs Kemp in the right direction. She walked up the hospital corridor and found the room she was looking for.

"Hello, Mrs O'Driscoll," she said. "How's our patient doing today?"

"As well as can be expected," Mrs O'Driscoll replied. "Still asleep," she smiled, nodding at the figure in the hospital bed.

"Would you like a break?" said Mrs Kemp. "I'm happy to sit here for a couple of hours, and then I think Mr Jermyn's coming up to visit, too."

Mrs O'Driscoll looked at the sleeping patient.

"Thanks, Mrs Kemp," said Mrs O'Driscoll. "It's been three days since the accident, but my nerves are still shaking."

"We can only thank goodness that no one was killed or seriously injured," sighed Mrs Kemp, shaking her head.

"I think we have someone else to thank," said Mrs O'Driscoll. She nodded towards the bed. "Our friend, Old Bob."

By now, all of Southwold knew the incredible story. When the ambulances and the fire service had arrived on the scene, they'd found all the passengers, sore and bruised, but safe. The minibus had been reduced to a smoking wreck by the fire that had spread through it, and a sullen spire of smoke drifting up through the drizzle was all that remained of the blaze.

One by one, the ambulance crews had hauled stretchers up the ravine to the roadside, where paramedics carefully checked each of the children.

Then, one of the fire officers who had struggled down to the burnt-out minibus, had yelled out.

"There's someone here!" he had shouted. "Bring a stretcher down."

They'd found Bob, clasping his supermarket bag, barely breathing. The minibus had erupted into a ball of flame just as he'd squeezed himself out of the smashed door one last time.

For the last three days, he'd been recovering in hospital. And, as the story of Old Bob's heroism was gradually put together from the stories of the children, Miss Penfold and Mr Finlay, Mrs O'Driscoll became the first and most frequent visitor among the stream of grateful parents and teachers who kept a vigil by his bedside.

Mrs O'Driscoll went in search of a cup of tea. Alone in the ward, Mrs Kemp looked at Old Bob. Among the flowers and cards from well-wishers, she noticed the old supermarket bag. Even half-conscious, Old Bob had refused to be parted from it.

"Why would you risk your life for an old supermarket bag?" she said to herself, shaking her head. "I've only ever seen you drag old chocolate out of it. Surely you wouldn't go back for that?"

Mrs Kemp stood up and looked over her shoulder. Hoping a passing nurse wouldn't catch her, she guiltily walked over to Old Bob's bedside cabinet and picked up the supermarket bag. She wrinkled her nose and looked inside.

"Scraps of newspaper?" she said, puzzled. "Why would you keep old newspapers?"

Mrs Kemp gingerly pulled a lump of melted chocolate off the edge of one of the pieces of paper and looked at it more closely. Then she sat down. She could scarcely believe her eyes.

HOLIDAY BUS TRAGEDY

A bus carrying families to a seaside vacation has plunged down a ravine near Crestwick. Despite being badly injured, a young passenger managed to pull many survivors to safety. Tragically, the seven-year-old boy known only as "Young Bob" learnt after the crash that his parents had perished. Authorities say that the boy will be taken into care.

Mrs Kemp looked at the date on the newspaper. 30 January 1966. "Oh, Bob," she said, tears welling up in her eyes. "That's why you never finished school."

The story of Old Bob's double heroism was big news. When he was well enough to sit up, he found himself surrounded by TV cameras and journalists pushing microphones at his whiskery face.

"I just did what anybody would have done," he muttered, looking embarrassed and trying to avoid the cameras. "Again."

Old Bob couldn't wait for all the fuss to die down.

A couple of weeks later, Old Bob was released from hospital. A taxi was waiting for him, and the driver whisked him straight to Southwold School.

Mr Jermyn, Miss Penfold, Mrs Kemp, his classmates and their parents had all gathered to give him a hero's welcome.

"It's good to see you back," smiled Mr Jermyn, after everyone had shaken Old Bob's hand and patted

him on the back. He gently steered Bob through the crowd of well-wishers towards the caretaker's shed.

"I hope you're still interested in the caretaker's job," he said.

Bob nodded and smiled at Mr Jermyn and the rest of the school community.

"Sorry I couldn't start when you wanted me to," he said. "I promise I'll be on time from now on."

Mr Jermyn laughed. He pointed to a sign above the shed door.

"Our friend Bob," read Old Bob out loud. "Thanks, Mr Jermyn."

"Oh, and Bob," added Mr Jermyn, above the clapping of the crowd. "There's just one more thing. Do you remember that when we first met I said you had to follow the rules? My rules."

A look of concern crossed Old Bob's face. "Yes, Mr Jermyn," he said.

"Well, here's another one," said the principal sternly.

Old Bob looked worried.

Our Friend Bob

“No more bus trips. OK?”

Old Bob grinned sheepishly. “I’ll write that down so I don’t forget,” he said proudly.

“I’m sure you will,” said Mr Jermyn. “Thanks, Bob.”

Bob looked at the faces in front of him. He knew he still had a long way to go before he could read words as well as everyone else – but he could read faces and those in front of him were all saying the same thing.

“Thank you, Bob. Our friend, Old Bob.”